Will You Be My Friend?

For Leila and Neil, my first best friends

—S. L.

For Kimberly Porter

—M. H.

A FEIWEL AND FRIENDS BOOK

An Imprint of Macmillan

WILL YOU BE MY FRIEND?. Text copyright © 2016 by Parachute Publishing, LLC.

Photographs copyright © 2016 by Murray Head. All rights reserved.

Printed in China by RR Donnelley Asia Printing Solutions Ltd., Dongguan City, Guangdong Province.

For information, address Feiwel and Friends, 175 Fifth Avenue, New York, N.Y. 10010.

Our books may be purchased in bulk for promotional, educational, or business use.

Please contact your local bookseller or the Macmillan Corporate and Premium Sales Department

at (800) 221-7945 ext. 5442 or by e-mail at MacmillanSpecialMarkets@macmillan.com.

Library of Congress Cataloging-in-Publication Data is available.

ISBN 978-1-250-04643-7 (hardcover)

Book design by Anna Booth

Feiwel and Friends logo designed by Filomena Tuosto

First Edition—2016

1 3 5 7 9 10 8 6 4 2

mackids.com

Will You Be My Friend?

Susan Lurie

Photographs by Murray Head

Feiwel and Friends
NEW YORK

Can I tell you a secret?
Here it is—I am shy.
And I am quite worried.
Do you want to know why?

I need a friend,
and the trouble, you see,
will be finding a friend
for a shy guy like me.

This peacock's too fancy.

The frog is too jumpy.

This duck is too noisy.

That bird looks too grumpy.

Too busy.

Too hairy.

Too many.

Too scary.

"Mouse, stop your complaining,"
said that real grumpy bird.
"You want a friend?
Is that what I heard?

"Well, you already have one,
so listen to me.
Keep looking. You'll find him.
Hint: He lives in a tree.

"Now leave me alone.
I hate giving advice.
To anyone, really,
but mostly to mice."

I kept up my search
because the Grump said he knew
that I had a friend.
So I followed his clue.

I found a big owl.

We talked the whole day.

"Hoo hoo hoo hoo hoo."

That's all he would say.

It couldn't be him,

so I searched the next tree.

I saw a small squirrel,

but he was shyer than me.

"I can't find my friend.
Are you sure he is here?"
I asked that mean Grump,
who said, "Yes, he is near.

"Your friend is quite close.
That is hint number two.
I can see him right now.
That's the last hint for you."

Well, I saw a cute chick
who wanted his mother.

I saw two raccoons,
but they had each other.

"Grump, I've looked everywhere.
I've searched the whole day.
Not him, her, or them—
that's all you will say.

"I do not know what
you are talking about.
Where is this friend?
I can't figure it out."

"Mouse, you have a secret,
and I have one, too.
I may be real grumpy,
but I'm shy, just like you.

"So will you be my friend?"
The Grump spoke really fast.
"I was frightened to ask,
but I've asked it at last."

We played every day,
and in a short while,
I saw that his frown
was the same as his smile.

What a great surprise
to find in the end.
So I stopped calling him Grump.
Now I call him my friend.